Sometimes this book may roam free, so
here's how to get it safely back to me!

. . . .

. . . .

. . . .

. . . .

. . . .

. . . .

. . . .

. . . .

. . . .

. . . .

“How soon? How soon?”
wondered Little Herdy
one humdrum afternoon.
“How soon till I’m old enough?”

**“I’ve sped down the fellside
and climbed to the top
made loops around the family tree
and slid down the barn roof,
bop!”**

On this side of the heaf
there was nothing left to do,
so Little Herdy looked out
far across the view
and looked...
and looked...
until the view came to a stop.

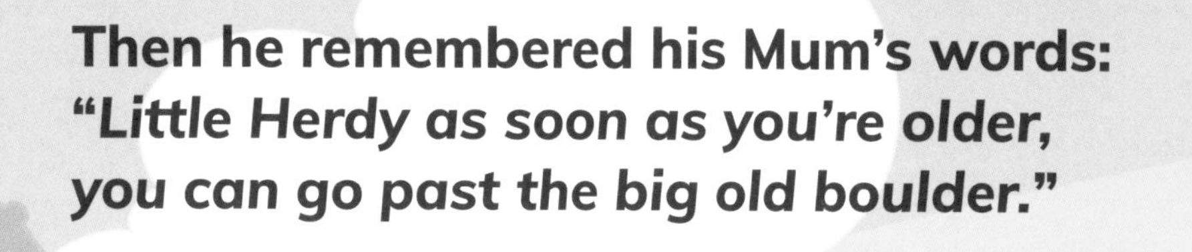

Then he remembered his Mum's words:
"Little Herdy as soon as you're older,
you can go past the big old boulder."

He jumped and skipped and stamped around.
"My muscles feel strong and tough.
It must be very, very soon
that I'll be old enough."

At Herdy school there are lots of classes
on grazing manners, woolly matters
and of course, P.E.
But the most important class to pass,
is Herdy-o-logy! (how to find their way home)

Now, humans might be experts on walking on two legs and drinking tea. But they don't know the first thing about Herdy-o-logy.

There are complicated calculations:
the slant of the hill, divided by the speed of the breeze.
Add the stars overhead to the distance around the tarn
and multiply the warm smells coming from the farm.

But the most important thing of all,
is a secret that's virtually unknown (shhhh...!)
A Herdy has an extra bone!
It works like a compass
and always points to home.

So, instead of doing another loop around the family tree, Little Herdy thought, "*I know, while Mum's asleep I'll tiptoe off and explore the rest of the heaf!*"

**And there he met the big old boulder
that was way bigger and way bolder
than any boulder should probably be.**

"Hey Old Mr Boulder," Little Herdy said.
"I've played all over this side.
I'm sure I'm more than ready now
to go past your big grey shoulders."

But there was no answer...

"Hello?"

"Can I go?"

There was still no answer…

So Little Herdy gave him a nudge
but the big old boulder wouldn't budge.
He just looked at Little Herdy
with his deep set eyes
in his suit made of moss
and said, "*no passing till you're older!*"
in his deep and rumbling voice.

Now,
between Little Herdy and the boulder,
well,
the boulder was obviously the boss.

"Okay Old Mr Boulder," said Little Herdy,
"since you're fixed on staying here,
let me pass and when I return
I'll tell you everything I've learned."

And the big old boulder didn't disagree
and didn't get in his way,
and that's how Little Herdy was sure
their arrangement was okay.

So, what did Little Herdy find when he
peeped around Old Mr Boulder?

A whole new fell side
to play in and explore!
"*Baa baa baaaa baa ba!*" he exclaimed.
"*I'm the new Herdy on this heaf!*"

He raced a jackdaw
splashed in the beck
bounced on the boing-y moss
and watched the clouds
while a worm stretched its neck.

**But before Little Herdy noticed,
it began to grow dark
and the dandelion clocks flew past
reading late o'clock.**

"Uh oh!" thought Little Herdy,
his ears sunk right down.
"I'm out all on my own
and can't remember the way home."

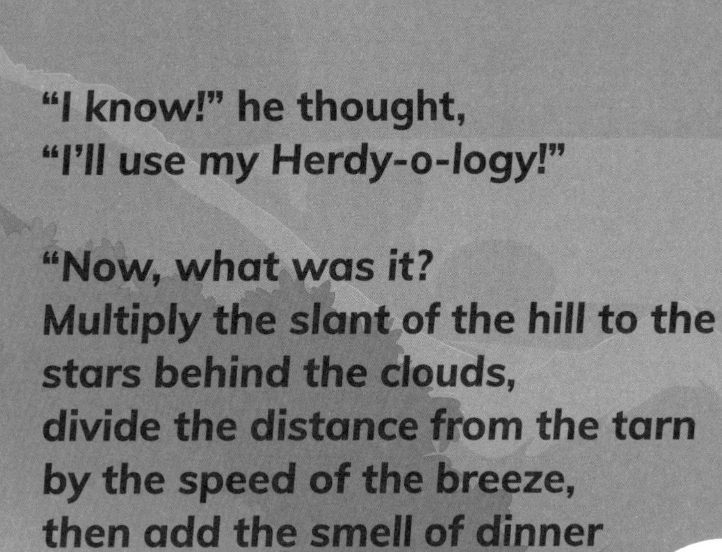

"I know!" he thought,
"I'll use my Herdy-o-logy!"

"Now, what was it?
Multiply the slant of the hill to the
stars behind the clouds,
divide the distance from the tarn
by the speed of the breeze,
then add the smell of dinner
coming from the farm..."

"Oh no!" frowned Little Herdy,
giving himself a fright.
For no matter how hard he tried,
he couldn't get it right.

When suddenly,
an owl hooted "*looook looook*"
and a field waved "*hay hay*"
then a deer bolted right past
with spots that read, "*this way!*"

Everything seemed to point him
from one place to the next,
to the next and
to the next,

until he found himself standing
in front of... guess who?

"*Little Woolliby Herdy!*" said Mum crossly,
"*You have some explaining to do.*"

So Little Herdy told her the whole long yarn.

Mum asked, "*now what will you do next time you reach Old Mr Boulder?*"
Cheekily Little Herdy said,
"*I'll tell Old Mr Boulder all about the fell behind his shoulder!*"

"And?"

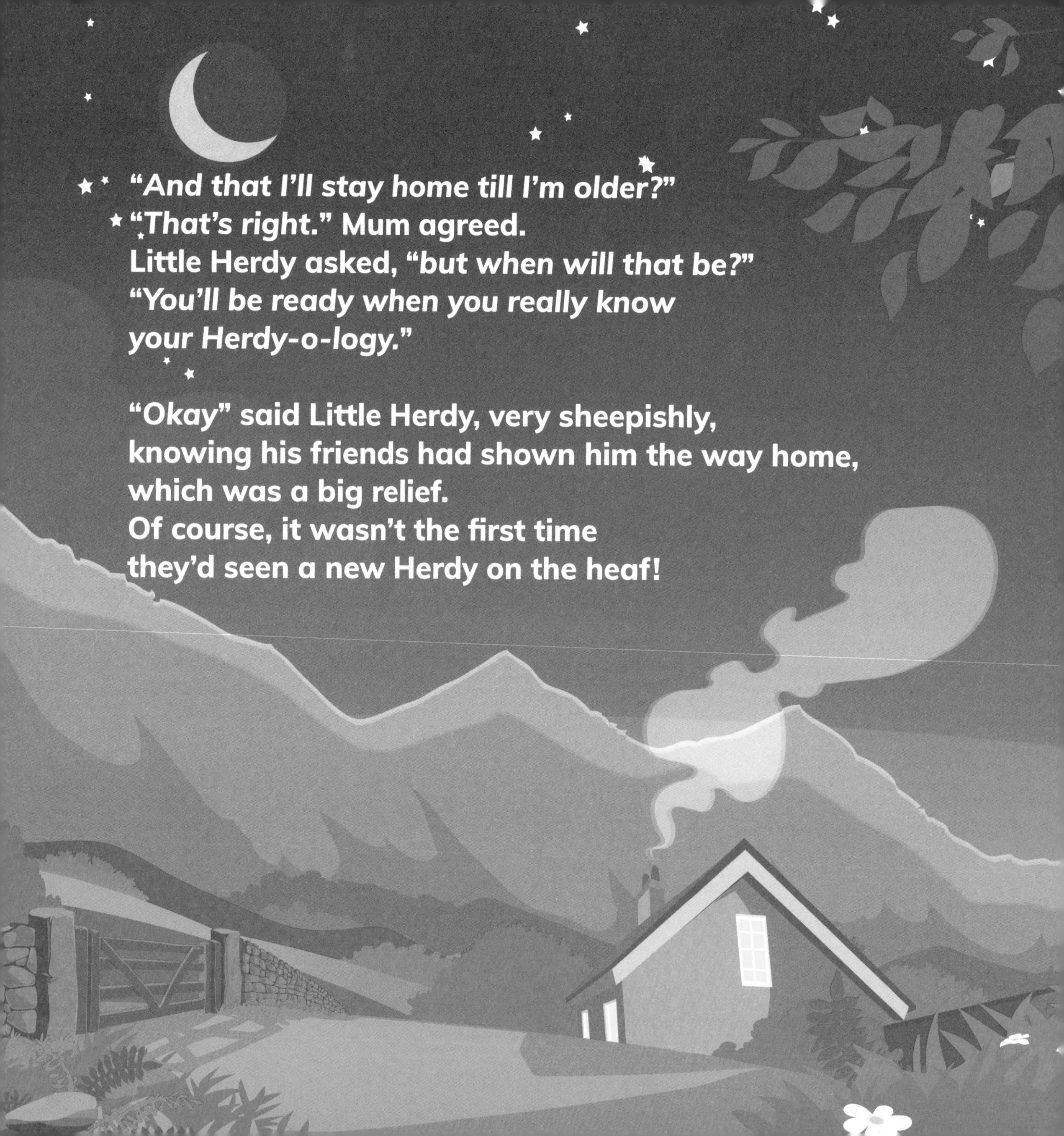

"And that I'll stay home till I'm older?"
"That's right." Mum agreed.
Little Herdy asked, *"but when will that be?"*
"You'll be ready when you really know your Herdy-o-logy."

"Okay" said Little Herdy, very sheepishly,
knowing his friends had shown him the way home,
which was a big relief.
Of course, it wasn't the first time
they'd seen a new Herdy on the heaf!

Herdy Dictionary of Terms

"Baa baa baaa baa ba"
"Wow, how super-dooper amazing great!"

Beck
A small river or stream.

Fell
The mountains and hills of the Lake District used by fell farmers as common grazing land.

Heaf
The special part of a fellside that Herdy calls home and returns to year after year.

Herdy-o-logy
The clever and secret science of how Herdy finds his way home.

Tarn
A little mountain lake made a long, long time ago by ancient, slow moving rivers of ice.

Yarn
An exciting story made of twists, loops, gasps and laughs.